# Bake a Wish

## Mend-It Muffins

*Lorna Honeywell*

Illustrated by Samantha Chaffey

**SCHOLASTIC**

*With special thanks to Pearl Morrison*

First published in the UK in 2012 by Scholastic Children's Books
An imprint of Scholastic Ltd
Euston House, 24 Eversholt Street
London, NW1 1DB, UK
Registered office: Westfield Road, Southam, Warwickshire, CV47 0RA
SCHOLASTIC and associated logos are trademarks
and/or registered trademarks of Scholastic Inc.

Text copyright © Hothouse Fiction Limited, 2012
Illustrations copyright © Samantha Chaffey, 2012

The right of Lorna Honeywell and Samantha Chaffey to be
identified as the author and illustrator of this work has been asserted by them.
Produced by Hothouse Fiction.
www.hothousefiction.com

Cover illustration © Katie May Green, 2012

ISBN 978 1 407 13481 9

A CIP catalogue record for this book is available
from the British Library.

Printed and bound by CPI Group (UK) Ltd, Croydon, CR0 4YY
Papers used by Scholastic Children's Books are made from
wood grown in sustainable forests.

1 3 5 7 9 10 8 6 4 2

www.scholastic.co.uk/zone

*For Kitty Morrison, also affectionately*

*known as Granny Orkney.*

# 1

## Trouble in the Garden

It was a warm summer afternoon and school had finished for the day. Lily Dalton skipped happily as she followed Grandma home. She and her little brother Archie went to Grandma's house every day after school until their mum and dad finished work. Archie was racing ahead, swinging his rucksack in front of him. It was such a beautiful day – Lily couldn't help feeling happy!

"Why don't we go and do some painting in the garden?" Grandma suggested as they went inside.

"Yes, please!" Lily grinned.

"Yeeeaah!" Archie yelled.

Grandma went indoors, then reappeared with a box. Inside were paints, brushes and some paper. As well as suncream and hats for Lily and Archie.

"You need to put some cream on, or you'll be as pink as Lily's sun hat!" Grandma joked as she rubbed the cream on to Archie's wriggly legs and arms.

Lily put her cream and her pink sun hat on, and then she settled down on the grass and was soon painting a picture of the tall sunflowers growing next to Grandpa's shed. Grandma sat with her, helping to mix the colours. Archie started hunting for bugs in the hedge. The garden was so peaceful and quiet that the only sounds were Grandpa digging in the vegetable patch and a bee buzzing in the flowers.

But then Lily heard an extra loud "*bzzzzzzzzzzz!*" She looked up. Archie was chasing a bee across the grass. His arms were outstretched just like a pair of wings and he was making a buzzing sound.

As the bee flew closer, Lily covered her head with her arms. "I don't like bees!" she cried. "They sting!"

"It won't hurt you," Grandma told her. "It thinks your painting is a real flower." But the bee didn't land on Lily's painting. It sailed over her head and flew towards the sunflowers.

Archie came chasing after it, running so close to where Lily was sitting that he almost stood on the edge of her painting.

"Careful, Archie," Grandma told him.

"Sorry," Archie gasped. He looked very hot. His face was red and shiny under his cap.

"It's much too warm to be running around," Grandma told him. "Why don't you do some painting?"

Archie shook his head and took a deep breath. "I'm . . . going to catch . . . the bee."

Lily watched him race across the garden.

"The bee will sting you," she warned. But Archie wasn't listening.

Lily went back to finishing her painting. "I'm going to give it to Mum and Dad as a present," she told Grandma happily. Sunflowers were her mum's favourite flower.

"What a lovely idea," Grandma smiled.

Lily was dipping her brush into the yellow paint when she heard feet running towards her again.

"Look out!" Archie teased, racing nearer. He flapped his arms and laughed. "Help! I can't stop!"

Lily quickly picked up her painting and held it safely. "Go away! Stop being a pest!" Archie tilted his arms and changed direction, but his foot knocked against the jam jar and it toppled over. There was a swishy gurgling sound as water poured on to the grass. Not a drop was left in the jar.

"Oh, Archie!" Lily said crossly. "Now I can't wash my brushes!"

Grandma picked up the empty jar. "Archie," she said. "Why don't you help Grandpa pick some peas in the vegetable patch?"

Archie shook his head. "I'm a bee! Bees don't like peas. *Bzzzzzzzzz*," he added, and set off again. He ran round the vegetable patch and rushed past Grandma's cat, Hector, who was asleep on the doorstep. Hector got such a fright that he jumped up with a surprised meow. Grandma's two chickens, Bessie and Jessie, clucked and flapped their wings as Archie charged past the coop.

"Slow down, Archie," Grandpa told him.

Lily added the last bit of paint to her sunflower painting and she held it up to show Grandma. "I've finished," she said.

"Do you like it?"

"Oh, Lily!" Grandma told her. "It's lovely. Mum and Dad will be pleased."

Lily smiled. "Thank you! I think it's the very bestest painting that I've *ever* done." She laid it down on the grass to dry just as Archie came charging towards her again.

"Watch out!" Lily told him.

But Archie kept on running. He came faster and faster, closer and closer.

"Stop, Archie. Please!" Grandma told him.

Archie quickly swerved away. "Only joking!" he laughed as he ran past. His feet just missed the painting, but the grass was wet where he had knocked over the water and he started to slip. He waved his arms around trying to stop himself from falling, but he couldn't. "Ouch!" he said as he landed on the ground with a bump.

Lily gasped.

"Oh no," Grandma sighed.

Archie sat up and smiled at them. "It's OK. I'm not hurt," he grinned.

But Lily burst into tears. Archie's hand had landed on her lovely artwork and crumpled it up.

There were two big rips down the middle.
"Look what you've done!" she wailed.
"My lovely sunflower painting is ruined!"

## Disaster!

Archie lifted his hand up from Lily's painting. "Oops!" he said.

Lily wiped the tears from her eyes. "You've *torn* my picture! It was a present for Mum and Dad," she sobbed.

"Oh, Lilybee!" said Grandma as she gave her a hug. "Don't cry."

Archie gulped and pointed to the damp ground. "It was an accident. I slipped."

Lily glared at him. "It was NOT an

accident! You kept running around. Grandma told you not to!"

Archie looked at the torn painting and then he looked at her with his bottom lip wobbling. "Maybe you could paint another one?"

Lily grabbed her painting. "This one was *perfect*! It took me ages and ages! Now it's spoiled!"

Archie got to his feet and wiped mud and grass from his hands. "Sorry, Lily."

"You're not sorry *at all*," Lily shouted. She turned to Grandma. "He's not sorry, is he, Grandma?"

"Yes, I am," Archie insisted. "I am!"

Grandma put the paintbrush in the paint box and closed the lid. "Time to go indoors," she said. "I think you've both had too much sun."

"This is all *your* fault," Lily told Archie.

"You ruined my painting and now we have to go inside!"

Archie's bottom lip wobbled even more. "It was a rubbish painting anyway!" he shouted.

Lily jumped up and put her hands on her hips. "Better than the squiggles you do!"

Archie puffed out his chest. His forehead creased into a big frown and he looked like he was about to cry. But Lily was too cross to mind that her little brother was upset.

"Well, you're rubbish at *everything*!" he replied.

"And you are the most horriblest person in the whole world!" Lily yelled.

As Archie and Lily got noisier and noisier, Bessie and Jessie, Grandma's chickens, started clucking and flapping their wings. Even Grandpa stopped digging.

"Hey, you two," he called, picking a pea pod and holding it up. "I need some *peas* and quiet."

Lily didn't laugh. "It's all Archie's fault," she called back. "He ruined my painting!" She held it up to show Grandpa the ripped paper.

Archie glared at her. His fists were clenched and his bottom lip was stuck out in a pout. "It was an *accident*!" he yelled. "I *said* sorry."

Lily threw her painting to the ground. "You always mess up everything, Archie!"

Archie opened his mouth ready to argue back.

"*Stop!*" Grandpa said firmly, raising his hand up like a traffic policeman. Lily and Archie looked at him. "Archie," he said. "You got a bit silly and ended up spoiling Lily's hard work, but it was an accident. Lily, I think you should accept his apology."

Lily folded her arms and shook her head.

Archie folded his arms, too. "I'm not saying sorry again."

Grandma sighed. She gathered up the paint box and the empty jam jar. "Maybe a nice cool drink will make things better."

Lily picked up her torn painting. The only thing that would make her better was if her painting wasn't ruined. She followed Grandma back to the house, stomping along behind Archie. *I am never going to speak to him ever again*, Lily thought as she pushed her painting into the bin.

Inside the kitchen, Grandma opened the fridge and took out a cold bottle of lemonade while Lily and Archie stood apart and watched grumpily. There was just enough for two glasses with a little left over. The lemonade fizzed and bubbled as Grandma poured it out.

Lily licked her lips excitedly – she couldn't wait to taste it! She took a sip and the icy-cold bubbles rushed up her nose. "Aahhhh," she sighed. All the hot and bother she felt was starting to fade away.

She was still annoyed at Archie, but not quite as much.

"I'm so thirsty," Archie gasped. He finished his drink and poured the last of the lemonade into his glass.

Lily looked at the empty bottle and gave an angry wail. "You've taken it all!"

Archie gulped down the lemonade. His eyes were wide as he stared at Lily over the top of his glass. When he was finished he licked his lips and said, "I was thirsty."

"So was I!" Lily argued. She turned to Grandma. "First Archie ruined my picture and now he's taken all the lemonade. It's so unfair!" She glared at Archie. "You *know* lemonade is my favourite drink."

Grandma sighed. "There's only one way to stop all this squabbling."

Archie gave a small bubbly burp. "More lemonade?"

"No," said Grandma. "I'm afraid that was the last bottle."

Lily gave a disappointed sigh and flopped down on a chair. She felt like crying.

"But I know just the thing to cheer

you both up," Grandma declared. She walked over to the dresser and reached up to a white and yellow stripy jar on the top shelf.

Lily sat up and her tummy gave an excited little flip. The white and yellow stripy jar meant only one thing. They were going to make magic!

# 3

## Making a Wish

At last Lily felt like smiling. Grandma's white and yellow stripy jar might look ordinary, but Lily knew it was extra special. It always helped whenever she or Archie had a problem. It had cured Archie's bad mood when he couldn't do his numbers and it had given Lily the confidence to sing in the Easter Show. It had even helped their cousin Izzy to stop being afraid of the dark. All they had to do was make a wish, and a recipe and some baking ingredients would magically appear inside it. And now the jar was going to help Lily again, just when she needed it!

*What magical recipe will be in the jar today?* she wondered. She couldn't wait to find out. "Hurry, Grandma!" she smiled.

Sunshine was pouring in through the window as Grandma carried the jar to the table. Hector rubbed his tail against her legs and gave a friendly purr. Then his collar bell rang as he jumped up on a chair next to Lily at the table.

Lily smiled at him and stroked his ears. Hector always liked to watch them bake.

Grandma set the jar down on the table. Lily felt all tingly inside, as if she were full of magic.

"Can I make the wish?" Archie asked Grandma. He looked at her with wide pleading eyes.

"No!" Lily jumped up from her chair. "I should get to make it," she told Grandma. "It was *my* painting that got ruined!"

Archie crossed his arms and frowned.

Grandma sighed. "I think you each need a little magic," she said. "You can *both* make a wish. One at a time!" she added, as they rushed to put their hands on the jar.

Archie went first. He put his hand on the jar and closed his eyes, just as he did when he blew out birthday candles.

He whispered his wish so quietly that Lily couldn't hear it. *He's probably wishing something mean about me*, she thought grumpily.

And then it was Lily's turn to make a wish. She knew exactly what it would be. She closed her eyes and touched the jar. *I wish my painting was mended and Archie would stop being so annoying so that we could be friends.*

Lily opened her eyes. Archie was now jumping up and down and tugging Grandma's apron. "Let me open the jar!" he begged.

Lily sighed. Her wish hadn't come true yet – Archie was *still* being annoying! "I should get to open it," Lily snapped at him.

They both reached for the jar at the same time, but Grandma got there first.

"I'll open it," she said. "That way there will be no arguments."

Grandma started to pull off the lid.

Lily and Archie leaned forward, eager to peer inside.

"I wonder what's in it this time?" Lily whispered to Grandma.

"I hope there's chocolate," Archie said.

"Mmmmm!" Lily agreed.

Grandma lifted the lid and held the jar out to Lily. She dipped her hand inside and brought out . . . bananas.

Lily liked bananas when they were bright yellow and fresh, but these two were horrible and brown. She couldn't hide her disappointment.

Archie wrinkled his nose. "They don't look very nice," he said.

"Don't worry," Grandma told them. "They're very soft, which makes them perfect for baking with."

Then it was Archie's turn to reach inside the jar. He pulled out a bag of chocolate chips. His eyes lit up. "Yum, that's better!" He peered back inside the jar. "That's all the ingredients." He looked at Grandma. "What can we make with old bananas and chocolate chips?"

"The recipe will tell us," Lily said. She put her hand in the jar and moved it around until she found the white piece of paper right at the bottom. As always, there wasn't a title on the recipe. She held it out to Grandma. "What is it we're going to make this time?"

Grandma read out all the ingredients they would need. "Bananas . . . chocolate chips . . . flour . . . butter . . . sugar . . . milk." She looked surprised. "Well, well, well," she smiled.

"What is it?" Lily asked. Her tummy was making excited little flips again.

Grandma smiled at them. "This recipe is for Mend–It Muffins!"

"Mend–It Muffins?" Archie stared in amazement at the magic jar. "Will they mend Lily's painting?" he asked.

"Maybe," Grandma smiled. "We'll just have to make the delicious muffins to find out."

Archie poked a banana with his finger. "How can brown bananas be delicious?"

"That's part of the magic of baking," Grandma said, pointing to their hands. Archie's were covered with dirt from where he'd fallen over, and Lily's were splattered with yellow paint. "But what do we need to do first?"

"Wash our hands!" Archie and Lily cried as they hurried over to the sink. Lily turned on the tap and began to rinse the paint from her fingers. She watched Archie pump soap on to his muddy palms and send bubbles floating up from his fingers. He was still washing his hands by the time Lily had put her cupcake apron on.

"Wait for me! I'm not ready!" he said.

But Lily didn't want to wait. If they were making muffins, then they would need cake cases, and she wanted to choose them without any argument from Archie.

She opened the door to the Yummy Cupboard. It was one of her favourite places. It was difficult to be in a bad mood when you were surrounded by shelves of nice baking things. There were birthday candles and cake sprinkles and bottles of flavourings and chocolate sauce.

Lily breathed in slowly through her nose. The cupboard always smelled different each time she went inside. Today she could smell toffee and strawberry ice cream. The smell was so delicious she forgot all about her argument with Archie.

Lily crouched down and looked at the packets of cake cases on the bottom shelf. There were so many to choose from. Rainbow-coloured ones, stripy ones with little frills around the edge and heart-shaped ones.

"We'll need big cases for the muffins, Lily," Grandma called as she put the oven on to warm up.

"OK!" Lily yelled back. She already knew exactly which ones she wanted – the flower-patterned ones that had bluebells, daffodils, poppies and even sunflowers on! As she spotted them at the bottom of the box she smiled. *These are perfect.* If she couldn't give Mum and Dad a sunflower painting, she could give them a muffin in a sunflower case.

"What are you doing?" Archie asked. He was standing at the cupboard door wearing his dinosaur apron. Lily pretended not to hear him.

"Grandma asked me to get the flour and sugar," Archie told her, standing on his tiptoes and stretching for the pink and white bag of flour. Lily didn't help, but just picked up the cake cases, stuck her nose in the air and marched past him.

When Lily got back to the table, Grandma was busy laying out bowls and spoons on the kitchen table. Lily showed her the cake cases she had chosen. Grandma smiled and said, "Lovely choice, Lily. Why don't you put them in the tray?" She pointed to a baking tray with deep holes in it, perfect for cooking fairy cakes and muffins. Lily was carefully putting a cake case in each hole when Archie brought the flour and the sugar to the table. He pointed to the bluebell-patterned cake case.

"I want the muffin that goes in that one," he said.

"It's rude to say, 'I want'," Lily told him. "You should say, 'I would *like* that muffin, *please*'."

"They're not *your* muffins!" he grumbled.

"You're not eating them all!"

"Well, you're not getting *any* if you're going to be rude!"

Grandma sighed and shut her eyes. "No more arguing, *please*! Baking is supposed to be fun!" she told them. "Take a deep breath, both of you."

Lily and Archie both took a deep breath.

"Now blow all that grumpiness away," Grandma told them.

They both blew out hard. Lily wasn't sure if all the grumpiness was gone but she did feel a little better. Archie took another deep breath so that his cheeks swelled up and he blew out noisily.

"You can stop now," Grandma laughed. "Are you ready to bake?"

"Yes," they said together.

Grandma pointed to the two bowls on the table. "I think it might be more fun if you both have your own jobs to do. Lily, please can you mix the wet ingredients together? And Archie? I would like you to mix the dry ingredients."

Lily looked at Archie. He seemed as puzzled as she felt.

"What are wet and dry ingredients?" Lily asked.

"The wet ingredients are the eggs and milk," Grandma explained. "The dry ingredients are the flour and sugar. OK?"

They nodded.

Grandma smiled. "Then let's begin."

## Busy Bees!

The first thing Lily did was to look again at the Mend-It Muffins recipe. "It says I need to mix two eggs and half a cup of milk." She ran over to the fridge to get them out. The eggs were nice and brown and a bit dirty because they had been laid by Grandma's chickens, Bessie and Jessie.

Lily had baked with Grandma enough times now to know just what to do. She gently cracked the eggs against the side of the bowl just as Grandma had shown her. Then, using her thumbs, she broke the shells open. Two perfectly round yellow yolks slid down to the bottom of her bowl.

Lily mixed the eggs up with a fork. When they were all runny, she added half a cup of milk to the bowl and then began to whisk everything together.

Grandma was helping Archie measure out the flour on to the scales. When they had the right amount, she placed her big sieve over Archie's mixing bowl. With her help Archie poured in the flour and gently shook the sieve until a soft white shower drifted down through the tiny holes.

Archie looked at Lily and smiled. But she looked away, thinking to herself, *I am not ready to smile at you just yet.*

"Hmm, our recipe needs butter," Grandma said. "But it's been in the fridge, so it's a bit too hard to use. We'll melt it in the microwave to save time." She put the butter in a dish, covered it and popped it in the microwave for a few minutes.

Then she opened the kitchen windows and a gentle breeze floated in.

Lily glanced up from her whisking to see Grandpa pushing the wheelbarrow out in the garden. "Grandpa must be very thirsty," Grandma said. She poured out a glass of water. "I'll take a cold drink out to him."

"What about the butter?" Lily said as the microwave beeped.

"It's a wet ingredient, so we'll add it to your bowl," Grandma said, as she put on her oven gloves and lifted the dish out of the microwave. She poured the melted butter into Lily's bowl carefully. "Make sure to mix it in well. And no arguing while I take Grandpa a glass of water!"

With Grandma out in the garden, the kitchen was very quiet. Lily and Archie didn't look at each other and they didn't speak. Lily gently whisked the eggs, butter and milk. Archie shook the sieve a little harder. "I'm going to finish sieving before you finish mixing," he whispered.

"It's not a race, Archie," Lily said firmly. But she whisked the eggs and milk a little bit quicker. Round and round went her whisk, turning the mixture frothy.

Archie started to shake the sieve even faster. Little white clouds of flour landed all over his hands and spilled on to the table. Some even landed on Hector's nose. The cat gave a little sneeze.

"Stop it, Archie." Lily told him as she stirred faster and faster. She stirred so fast that the eggy mixture splashed on to her hands and hair.

"No, *you* stop it," Archie said, shaking the sieve so hard that more clouds of flour flew up into the air. When Lily saw that he was nearly finished, she whisked so fast yellow frothy waves started to swish around in her bowl but she couldn't slow down, not if she wanted to win. She kept whisking and stirring and Archie kept sieving so fast they were almost out of breath when at last Archie held up his sieve and shouted, "I won!"

Lily scowled. "No, you haven't!" She pointed to the sieve. "There's still some flour stuck to the bottom of it." Then she pointed to the scales. "And you haven't even added the sugar! It's a dry ingredient! Grandma asked you to mix the dry ingredients!"

"No," he insisted. "I just had to sieve the flour!"

Lily was about to reply, when bee that had been flying around the garden sailed in through the open window. "*Bzzzzzzzz*," it said as it swooped and buzzed above Lily's head.

"It's going to sting me!" she squealed, and ducked down under the table.

Archie raised the sieve above his head as if it were a butterfly net, and the last of the flour drifted down from it on to his hair. "Don't worry. I'll catch it and take it outside. Come here, Mr Bee," he called out. He climbed up on a chair to try and reach the bee, but it flew across the kitchen again.

Archie jumped to the floor, leapt over Hector's basket and swung the sieve. "Charge!" he shouted as he chased the bee.

When the bee landed on the table, Archie tried climbing up on a chair. He held on to the chair with one hand and swung the sieve with the other, but the bee was too quick for him. It flew straight through the open window and out into the garden.

"Come back!" he shouted. "Where are you going?"

The bee didn't reply, but a shocked voice did. "Archie!" Grandma gasped. "What *are* you doing?"

## 5

## A Mixing Mess

Grandma was standing in the kitchen doorway. Her mouth was open wide. She was staring at the flour in Archie's hair and on his face.

He smiled at her. "A bee was in here, Grandma." He waved the sieve around his head. "I was trying to catch it."

Lily climbed out from under the table. "Is the bee gone?" she asked. A strand of hair was stuck to her cheek with egg. "Yuck!" she said as she wiped it away. Then she saw Grandma's shocked face. "We've mixed the wet and dry ingredients!" she smiled.

Grandma didn't smile back. Instead she looked at the mess spilled on the table. "So I see. Is there any left in the bowl?" she asked, taking the sieve from Archie's hand and putting it in the sink.

"Baking needs exact amounts," she explained. "That's why we measure and weigh everything. If you spill too much of the ingredients, the muffins might not cook properly."

"Oh," said Archie.

He looked worried.

"Oh," said Lily.

She stared at the messy bowl of eggs.

"Does it mean we can't make the Mend–It Muffins?"

"It should still be OK," Grandma said, looking at the bowls. "But we have to take extra care when we bake."

"Sorry, Grandma," Lily mumbled.

Archie glanced at the flour lying on the table. "Has the magic all been spilled?"

Grandma put her arms around Lily and Archie and pulled them in for a hug. "The magic is always there," she told them. "Set your bowls aside for the moment." She brought out a plate and two forks. "Why don't you use up some of your energy by mashing the bananas?"

The bananas were so soft it didn't take long to mash them. They added them to Lily's bowl and while she stirred them into her mixture, Archie added the sugar to his bowl of flour. This time he stirred it all together carefully, without spilling any.

Grandma smiled. "Perfect," she told him. "Now you need to make a well."

"What's a well?" Archie asked.

"It's a little hole to put the egg mixture in," Grandma explained. She showed Archie how to gently push the flour and the sugar aside with his spoon to make a hole.

"This is fun," he said. "It's like digging a sandcastle."

Grandma asked Lily to pour the wet mixture in to the well bit by bit while Archie stirred.

"It's very important to stir gently," Grandma told him. "It keeps the air in the mixture and that makes the muffins light and fluffy."

"Fluffy?" Archie laughed. "Like Hector?"

Lily and Grandma giggled. "Not that kind of fluffy," Grandma explained. "It just means that they're tasty, so they melt in your mouth!"

They had one last ingredient to add. Grandma lifted up the bag of chocolate chips. "Who wants to sprinkle the chocolate chips into the mixture and who wants to stir?" she asked. "No arguing. Remember, be kind to each other! Be nice."

Archie looked at Lily. "I would *like to* add the chocolate chips." he said, politely. He held the spoon out to Lily. "Would you *like* to stir?"

Lily liked stirring a lot. "Yes, please," she said, and took the spoon. "Thank you, Archie."

"You're welcome," Archie said with a little smile.

Grandma handed Archie the bag of chocolate chips. "It's easier to mix them in if they're added a bit at a time."

Archie poured some of the chocolate chips into the bowl. He waited patiently until Lily mixed them in and said, "Some more please, Archie."

"It's so nice to have a peaceful kitchen again," Grandma said as she sat down in her favourite chair and Hector jumped up on her lap for a stroke.

*It's the magic*, Lily thought to herself. *It's starting to make everyone happy.*

When it was time to pour the muffin mixture into the cake cases, Archie and Lily were still working together.

Lily waited while Archie filled a case with a spoonful of the sticky muffin mixture and then Archie waited while Lily took a turn. They did everything they could to make sure the Mend-It Muffins stayed magical and delicious.

"There," Lily sighed happily when all the cake cases were full.

"Well done," Grandma smiled, opening the oven and popping the tray inside. Just before she closed the door, Lily had one last peek at the muffins through the glass oven door. *Please be full of magic*, she wished as hard as she could.

Grandma put the timer on, then wiped her hands on her apron. "Let's wash up while the muffins bake. It won't take long to do if we all help."

"I like working as a team," Lily said. "Things get done faster and better when you work together."

"And it's more fun," Archie added,
carrying the wooden spoons
towards the sink.

Grandpa opened the back
door. "Well, it's nice and
quiet in here," he smiled.

"We've been making
Mend-It Muffins,"
Archie said as he hung
up his apron. "They'll
be ready soon."

"You *have* been
busy," said Grandpa. "I
think you both deserve
a glass of lemonade!"

Lily sighed. She
would *love* a glass of
cold lemonade, but
she couldn't have any.

"There's none left, Grandpa," she explained. "Archie drank it all."

Archie frowned. "No, I didn't! There was only a teensy weensy bit." His voice grew louder. "Only enough for three gulps!"

"There was more than that!" Lily insisted. Her voice grew louder, too. "Anyway, you should have shared it!"

"You had some!" Archie yelled back so loudly that Hector shot into his basket.

"Now you've upset Hector," Lily scolded Archie.

"You're *so* bossy," Archie told her.

Lily was very cross. "You are sooooooo annoying."

"Enough!" Grandma interrupted. Lily and Archie stopped shouting, but glared at each other. "I have something *very* important to say!"

Lily and Archie stopped arguing and

stared at her.

Grandma looked at each of them. "Are you both listening carefully?"

"Yes," they replied together.

Grandma took a deep breath. "If you promise to stop bickering. . ."

Lily nodded excitedly.

"Then I'll show you how to *make* lemonade."

# 6

## Dizzy Lemonade

"You can't *make* lemonade, Grandma," Archie laughed. "It's got bubbles in it. That's why you have to buy it from the shops."

"You're right, Archie," Grandma told him. "It won't have bubbles in it, but it is still lemonade. A long, long time ago, lemonade was made from just water, sugar and real lemons." Grandma winked. "I can even show you how to make *pink* lemonade."

Lily bounced on the spot. "I've never had pink lemonade!"

"Grandma makes the best pink lemonade," Grandpa said as he pulled off his gardening gloves. "It's delicious!"

"Is it easy to make?" Archie asked.

"It's very easy," Grandma told him. "We only need four ingredients." She held up her hand and started counting on her fingers. "Sugar, cranberry juice, water and lemon juice."

"I know where the sugar is," Archie said, setting off towards the Yummy Cupboard.

"I'll get the cranberry juice," said Lily. She opened the fridge and took out a carton of juice. From a little shelf in the fridge door she picked up a yellow squeezy bottle in the shape of a lemon. "I've got the lemon juice, too."

"What are we going
to make the lemonade
in?" Archie
asked. He set
the bag of
sugar down on
the table next to
the empty lemonade
bottle.

"We need a small
saucepan and a jug,"
Grandma said.

Grandpa found
a glass jug in the
cupboard next to the
teacups and put it
on the table.

Grandma put the small pan on the hob.
"I'm going to make a sweet syrup. All I
have to do is add sugar to boiling water."

While Grandma made the syrup, she asked Archie to pour more water into the jug. Once that was done, Lily added lemon juice from the yellow squeezy bottle. "Now put in the cranberry juice, please," Grandma said. "And stir it all together. Easy peasy!"

"Look how pretty and pink it is!" Lily said as she stirred it round and round.

"Can I taste it?" Archie asked.

"You can try a tiny bit," Grandma told him. "But you might not like it!"

Archie dipped a spoon into the jug and took a small sip.

"Is it delicious?" Lily asked.

Archie shook his head and screwed up

his face. He looked very funny. His eyes were tightly shut and his tongue was hanging out. "It tastes spiky!" he gasped.

Grandma laughed. "It's called *sour*, Archie. That's because we haven't added the sugar yet." She poured the syrup from the pan into the jug. "*Now* it'll be nice and sweet."

Lily stirred the pink lemonade round and round until all the syrup was mixed in.

Archie tasted it again. This time he smiled. "Much nicer," he said, and licked his lips.

Grandpa patted his head and then

laughed. "How did you get flour in your hair, Archie?" he asked.

"He was chasing the bee with the sieve," Lily said. "It was flying around in the kitchen."

"You shouldn't chase bees," Grandpa told Archie. "They work very hard carrying pollen from flower to flower. If they didn't do that, I wouldn't have lovely flowers in the garden. Bees are usually too busy to sting people, so you don't have to be scared of them."

"What's pollen?" Lily asked.

"It's the yellow powder in the middle of a flower," Grandpa explained.

Archie cupped his chin in his hands and looked very sorry for himself. "I made the bee unhappy and I spoiled Lily's painting." He gave a big sad sigh.

"Cheer up," Grandpa told him. "I'm sure

the bee is busy taking pollen to the flowers right now. Let's go outside and see if we can find him. And you can help me with a little job that needs doing."

Archie looked towards the oven. A lovely smell was filling the kitchen. Then he looked longingly at the jug of lemonade.

Grandma smiled. "We'll have the lemonade when the muffins are finished baking," she told Archie. "It needs to cool more anyway. We can't have warm lemonade. Why don't you go outside and help Grandpa?"

"I'll let you know when the muffins are ready," Lily said. "We won't eat any without you, promise."

Archie followed Grandpa outside and Lily was left staring at the pink lemonade through the glass jug. "I wish I could drink it right now!" she said.

"Why don't you add some ice to the jug?" Grandma suggested. "That'll make the lemonade nice and cold."

Lily hurried over to the fridge and took a tray of ice cubes from the freezer. They were in the shape of little hearts. She added them to the lemonade and stirred. She watched the little hearts spin round and round, making a clinking sound as they bounced against one another. *Dizzy lemonade!* Lily couldn't wait to drink a whole glass. She was just putting in the last cube when the timer started to ring. Lily jumped up with excitement.

"It's such a lovely sunny afternoon," Grandma said, looking out of the window. "Why don't we take the muffins and the lemonade out to the garden and have a picnic?"

Lily clapped her hands. "Yes, please!"
A picnic was a brilliantly brilliant idea!

"Archie! Grandpa!" she called out to
the garden. "We're having a picnic!"

## Archie's Secret

Lily pulled on her sun hat and wandered into the garden, shading her eyes as she looked for her little brother. "Archie! Grandpa! Where are you?"

Hector trotted next to her, winding around her ankles. They walked up to the chicken coop but there was no sign of Grandpa and Archie there.

They weren't at the berry bushes either or watering the flower beds.

"Where are they, Hector?" Lily asked,

bending down to give him a stroke. Hector just purred.

Lily was on her way back to the house when she heard voices coming from the potting shed. She picked Hector up in her arms and walked quickly towards the shed. "They'll be so excited when I tell them we're having a picnic," she told him. Hector gave a happy *meow* as he bounced up and down in Lily's arms.

But when they reached the shed, Archie appeared in the doorway and blocked her way. "You can't come in," he said, stretching his arms wide.

"Why not?" Lily asked.

"Because it's just me and Grandpa who are allowed. We're doing a special job."

Lily tried to peer inside the shed. "What special job?"

Archie spread his arms wider. "Can't tell. It's a secret."

"Fine!" Lily said. "I don't care!" But she really did. She scowled at Archie. "Me and Hector are going to have a muffin and pink-lemonade picnic without you." And she stomped away. "Little brothers can be so annoying," she told Hector.

Hector looked up at her and gave a small *meow*. Lily kissed the top of his warm furry head. "Never mind about their silly old secret," she told him. "Let's go and get our picnic ready."

Grandma was already spreading an old tartan picnic rug out on the grass under the apple tree. Lily hurried over. She was so excited. She loved picnics. "Shall I bring the muffins out?" she asked.

"Yes, please," Grandma said. "We'll need plates too, and cups for the lemonade."

Lily set Hector down on the grass and skipped all the way to the house. The muffins had cooled down and Grandma had arranged them on a large blue plate. They looked lovely in their flowery bun cases. Lily made sure to set aside two muffins in sunflower cake cases for Mum and Dad before carrying the rest out into the garden.

Grandma followed with a basket of picnic cups and plates and the jug of lemonade. The ice cubes clinked and chinked in the jug as she walked.

There was a lovely delicious smell of warm muffins and melting chocolate. *This is magical*, Lily thought as she made herself comfortable on the rug and carefully peeled the case off a muffin. It was spongy and warm, with squidgy banana bits and melty chocolate chips. Lily took a bite and sighed happily. It was so lovely being in the speckly shade of the apple tree under the branches and leaves, with a delicious Mend-It Muffin to eat.

Lily lay down and gazed up at the blue sky. Little white wispy clouds were floating by. One of them looked just like a sunflower and another was just like a bee! She could hear real bees buzzing in the garden but she wasn't afraid of them any more because she knew that they were just being busy taking pollen to the flowers.

"Surprise!" someone said.

Lily sat up. Archie and Grandpa were standing in front of her. Archie was grinning and pointing down at the rug. There in front of her was her painting. Lily picked it up and looked at it closely.

"It's mended! My painting is mended." She looked at Grandma in amazement. "The Mend-It Muffins worked! My wish came true."

"It wasn't the Mend-It Muffins that did it," Archie said. He had a big smile on his face. "It was me!" he said proudly. "I fixed it with sticky tape and glue." He took Grandpa's hand. "That was our secret job in the shed! Grandpa helped me."

"You did a very good job, Archie," Grandma said. "You can hardly tell where the painting was ripped."

Lily couldn't stop smiling. "I'll be able to give it to Mum and Dad as a present after all!" She gave Archie a big hug. "Thank you."

"I'm sorry I tore your painting," he said. "It really was an accident."

"It's OK." Lily smiled. "I know you didn't really mean to."

"And I'm sorry I didn't share the lemonade with you."

"It doesn't matter. We've got lots of pink lemonade and yummy muffins! I'm sorry I got cross." Lily handed him the muffin in the bluebell case. "This one is especially for you."

Archie took one bite and sighed with delight. "Mmmm, it is fluffy and melty!"

"Yes," Grandma said. "Muffins made with teamwork and kindness always taste *extra* special." She smiled.

"Anyone for pink lemonade?"

"Yes, please!" said Archie, Lily and Grandpa all at the same time.

Grandma poured them all out cups of the pink lemonade and passed them around.

Lily took a long sip of her drink and closed her eyes. "Delicious!" she said. She licked her lips. "Cold and sweet."

Lily took another bite of her muffin. "Mmmmmmmm." It was so soft and light, it was just like eating a cloud.

She closed her eyes. The Mend-It Muffins really did taste magical. But were they? She suddenly remembered something. She opened her eyes. "Grandma? If Archie mended my picture, then my wish *didn't* come true. The Mend-It Muffins *weren't* magical after all!"

Grandma thought about it for a moment. Then she asked, "What did you wish for?"

"For my painting to be mended," Lily told her.

Archie sat up on to his knees. "That was my wish too!" he said. "That's why I wanted to make a wish! So your picture could be mended. *And* for us to be friends again!"

Lily gave a surprised smile. "I wished for that, too!"

Grandma kissed them both on the head. "Then the Mend-It Muffins *were* magical. They fixed things between you and Archie!"

"Hurray!" Archie said and gulped down the last of his drink. Lily watched him reach over and pick up the jug. There wasn't much lemonade left.

*Oh no!* Lily thought. *He's going to finish it all again!*

But Archie said, "Would you like some more lemonade, Lily?"

"Yes, please, Archie," she told him.

She watched Archie carefully pour the lemonade. *Plop!* A heart-shaped ice cube landed in her glass, and then another. Still Archie kept pouring until her glass was full. There was only a little left in the jug for him, but he didn't seem to mind. "This time, you can have the most lemonade, Lily," he said. "That means we're equal."

Lily smiled. Archie could be annoying sometimes, but she loved her little brother and she was pleased that they were friends again.

She felt so happy. Her painting was mended, the sun was shining and

she was having a perfect picnic with
Grandma, Grandpa, Archie and Hector.
It was magical.

Look out for more
Bake a Wish
books

# Bake a Wish

## Feel Good Fairy Cakes

Includes FANTASTIC cut-out-and-keep recipe card!

Lorna Honeywell

# Bake a Wish

## Can-Do Crispies

Includes
FANTASTIC
cut-out-and-keep
recipe card!

Lorna Honeywell

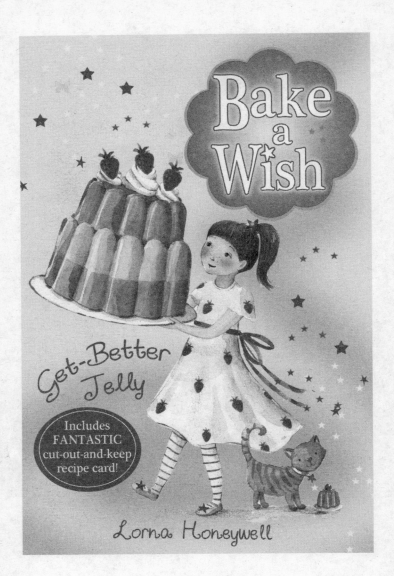

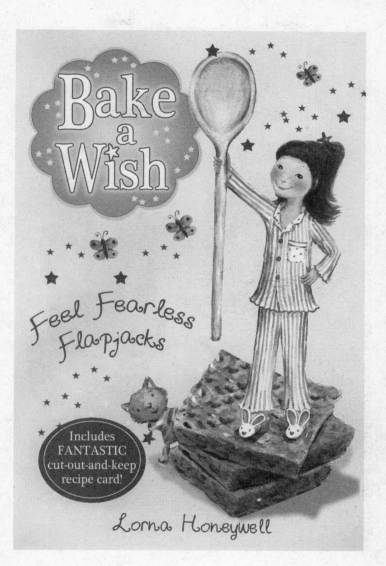

# Bake a Wish

## Feel Fearless Flapjacks

Includes FANTASTIC cut-out-and-keep recipe card!

Lorna Honeywell